Photo by Ken Nilssen

PETER BURCHARD is a professional writer and illustrator. He has illustrated close to 100 books, is author of *North by Night, Jed* (chosen as a Notable Book by the American Library Association), *Stranded: A Story of New York in 1875* and *One Gallant Rush* (a scholarly biography). His work has been widely acclaimed. The New York *Times* describes him as having "a splendid facility for characterization." He was a Guggenheim Fellow in 1966.

BIMBY grew out of his long-standing interest in American slavery and the anti-slavery movement. The story came to him while he was working on another book about an entirely unrelated subject. He says of BIMBY, "It was written out of love, not to meet a need. If it meets a need so much the better."

About the Book

The day was to have been a happy one for Bimby. He was going with Jesse to the white folks' picnic. Suddenly, without warning, happiness turned to nightmare.

BIMBY is the story of a day of decision in the life of a young slave in the Sea Islands of Georgia just before the Civil War. It is the story of a growing boy thrust toward manhood by an unforeseen event. Set against a background of light and darkness, it tells of simple pleasures, nagging fears, terror and its aftermath.

One-armed Jesse, who is old and kind, but deeply bitter; Bimby's mother, who sees slavery for what it is and yearns for freedom for her son; and Bimby himself are the central characters. Pierce Butler is "a good Massa"; Bucky is a cruel black man; Crazy Mary and Philip Washington are comic figures. All are three-dimensional, vivid, and unforgettable.

BIMBY, written with compassion and understanding, is a deeply moving portrayal of a dark side of American history.

BIMBY

BIMBY

BY PETER BURCHARD

COWARD-MCCANN, INC.   NEW YORK

Books by Peter Burchard

ADULT

One Gallant Rush: Robert Gould Shaw and
his Brave Black Regiment

JUVENILE

Balloons: From Paper Bags to Skyhooks

Jed

North by Night

Stranded

Bimby

Second Impression

© 1968 by Peter Burchard

Library of Congress Catalog Card Number: 68-23866
PRINTED IN THE UNITED STATES OF AMERICA

FOR LUCY

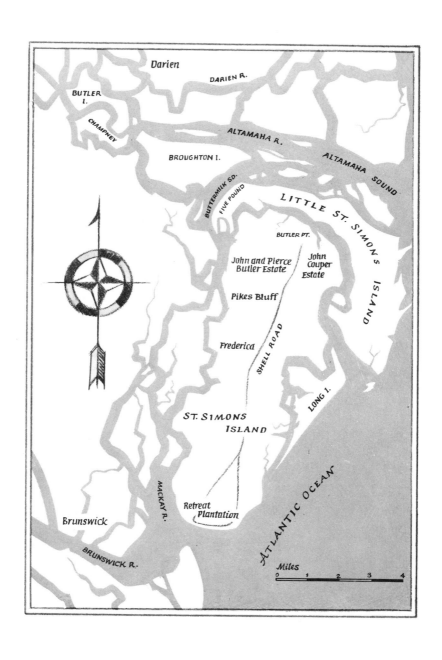

Darien

DARIEN R.

BUTLER I.

CHAMPNEY

ALTAMAHA R.

BROUGHTON I.

ALTAMAHA SOUND

BUTTERMILK SD.

FIVE POUND

LITTLE ST. SIMONS ISLAND

BUTLER PT.

John and Pierce Butler Estate

John Couper Estate

Pikes Bluff

SHELL ROAD

Frederica

LONG I.

ST. SIMONS ISLAND

MACKAY R.

Retreat Plantation

ATLANTIC OCEAN

Brunswick

BRUNSWICK R.

Miles
0   1   2   3   4

NOTE

This story is fiction set against a background of history. It takes place on the Butler plantations on the coast of Georgia before the outbreak of the Civil War. Except for Pierce Butler the characters are fictional.

BIMBY

1

That special Sunday started like most summer Sundays. It was quiet in the hut. Bimby had dozed after waking up. A gnat buzzed in his ear. He took a swipe at the gnat and looked out the doorway, squinting into the sun's glare. The mist had burned away early. He could see beyond the dike to the sparkling river and the fringe of dark pine on the shore of Champney Island. He rolled back to the middle of the cot, into the softness of the moss-filled bag that served as a mattress. No working in the rice fields today.

Bimby reached into a hole in the mattress and pulled out a dried corn cake he'd hidden there. He couldn't wait until noon for food. Wiley, who was bigger than Bimby, woke up, reached over and pretended to grab at Bimby's corn cake. Then he grabbed Bimby's foot and pulled as if to yank him out of bed. Bimby smiled. It never was bad being teased by Wiley.

Wiley dozed and Bimby lay back. He nibbled slowly at the corn cake, thinking. Beyond the landing and the river, beyond the fringe of pine and acres of marsh grass on the other islands, between here and the sea lay St. Simons Island, the place where Bimby had grown up, where his mother lived now. He'd lost his father when he was young. He couldn't even picture his face. Ma rarely talked about Pa and something made Bimby afraid to ask. Bimby didn't even know if his pa was alive. Pa had been a fine black-smith, Ma had said. She'd never told Bimby more than that. *Fifteen hundred dollars.* That was what old Jesse had said Pa was worth. That sounded like all the money in the world. It had made Bimby proud. But then Jesse had shut his mouth and looked away. Jesse made Bimby think that Pa had been sold.

Bimby listened and heard it in the distance, as if in answer to his thoughts, the faraway ringing of a blacksmith's hammer. Sometimes he imagined it was his father's hammer. And if he went to the forge his father would be there, and he'd smile at Bimby and say, "Good morning. What's your name, boy?"

Once, early in the morning, Bimby had followed the sound of the hammer. He'd been to the blacksmith's hut before but this was different. This time he'd thought it really *was* his father's hammer. He'd caught his breath as he approached the forge. The smith's broad back had been turned to Bimby, hard muscles working under moist, dark skin. The smith had turned to thrust a shoe into the furnace and his face had been the familiar face of a smith Bimby knew, young and alive in the light of the fire.

This morning such thoughts didn't make Bimby sad. Life had its weeping days and laughing days too. Even white folks had their weeping days. But today was the day of the great picnic when Massa and his friends, some from as far away as Savannah, would go by barge out to

19

St. Simons and pile into wagons for the long ride down to Retreat Plantation. There the feast would be spread on a bluff by the sea, Jesse had told him. There'd be music and dancing. The petticoats would fly. Likely nobody would weep today. The best part was that Bimby would be there. He and Jesse would row down into Buttermilk Sound and up into the Hampton River. And Bimby would see Ma in the evening. Jesse had promised.

2

Bucky, the fat cook's helper, stood in the doorway, black against the sky. He flicked his lash against the doorframe. Bucky's lash was thick like the man himself, a stout squarish leather thong bound to a lumpy wooden handle. Bucky said, "Git on out. Work to do."

The boys all scrambled for the door, all but Bimby and Alan. Bucky looked in again. Bimby sat up, ready to speak. Bucky's face was a leering mask. "Never mind talkin', jes git on out."

Bucky's glance traveled along the rows of cots. He saw Alan still asleep. "You . . ." he started.

Wiley was passing Bucky, going out the door. "That's Alan," he said. "Alan sick."

Bucky sneered. He'd come back later and poke Alan. He'd make sure he was sick. It took nerve to *play* sick. Bucky or the regular drivers, the ones who took them out to the rice fields, never spared the lash. If they didn't believe you, they'd lay it on good.

Bucky's cold pig eyes were on Bimby again. Bimby's heart sank. Bucky wouldn't even let him speak. Now he'd have to go with Bucky.

It was pretty good working at the cookhouse. But it was nothing compared to going home to St. Simons, nothing compared to the white folks' picnic.

Bucky gave the doorframe another whack. "Git on out. Don't try me, Bimby."

Bimby scrambled after the others. As he passed Bucky he breathed deep. But he couldn't get nerve up to speak to Bucky. Not now with Bucky's face hard as rock.

Bimby ran after the other boys, but he really wanted to run to Jesse's hut. Most times obedience came natural but now Bimby wanted to spit in Bucky's face, spit and fight back when Bucky swung his lash around. Bucky *knew* Bimby was supposed to go with Jesse. Bimby's heart pounded, not only from running but from being so mad.

Bimby fell into step beside the others. He looked at the ground, eyes riveted on the red-brown earth.

About halfway to the cookhouse, Bimby was aware that Bucky was near him, walking close. Bimby glanced sidelong and caught the glint in Bucky's eye. Bucky was just plain torturing him. A black man like Bucky was worse than any white man Bimby had known. He was proud of his belly, Bucky was. As he walked, he seemed to be holding it out, swinging it gently from side to side, making it keep time with the roll of his shoulders. And the devil was fast. Bimby had seen him chase a boy once. Seemed he always had to torture *some*body.

They didn't go into the cookhouse at all. The smells from inside drove Bimby crazy. They must be cooking things for the overseer's table. Corn muffins and bacon, smelled like. No black man ever ate like that. Bimby turned his face away from the door.

24

Bucky handed out spades and shovels. There were plenty of both to go around. The coopers saw to that. When they ran out of iron, they made them out of wood.

Bucky showed them where and they started digging. A garbage pit, that's what it was. Bimby and Wiley dug side by side. Bimby had a spade that was worn razor thin. He thrust it into the soft soil, pretended he was quartering Bucky's belly. He dug until he had to stop, put one foot on the edge of the hole and rested a moment, his hand wrapped loosely around the spade handle. He looked straight up into Bucky's eyes. This time he didn't even gulp. "Bucky, don't you remember? Massa said I could go with Jesse today."

"Massa didn't say that."

Bimby started to speak.

"Shut up, boy."

Bimby's lower jaw slid forward a little.

Then Bucky started to laugh. He laughed and slapped his belly. He wheezed and said breathlessly, "Massa said Jesse could take *one* boy. Massa didn't say it had to be you."

"He said which one was up to Jesse." Bimby took in a breath. "And Jesse chose me."

Bucky snickered. "Why, I know that, boy. I know that."

Bimby's lips were parted, but he didn't speak.

Bucky cocked his head on one side like a fat old hen. The other boys had stopped working. Bucky turned on them all, whacking the lash against his own leg. "Now, you boys git on back to your diggin'. I got to hear those shovels ring. Ring, shovels!"

He did a little one-footed dance. Nobody laughed at Bucky's antics. He stood still, his feet wide apart. "Now I tell you, Bimby," Bucky said, real pleased with himself. "You dug fast and furious. Now you can go join up with Jesse."

Bimby dropped his shovel and hopped up. He started walking. Bucky let him go quite a way. Then he called, "Come on back and pick up your shovel."

Bimby turned and walked slowly back to the pit. As he bent, he expected to feel Bucky's lash. He laid the spade at Bucky's feet.

This time Bucky didn't call him back. Bimby walked straight to the hut where he lived with the other boys. He fished under his mattress and brought out the shirt his ma had made him.

26

The shirt was bright red and almost new. He looked along the rows of cots. Alan slept. Sleep was better than digging a pit. Of course, maybe when they finished, the boys would have a turn at housekeeping chores; at least some of them might. Maybe they'd even have a nibble or two. A day away from the rice fields for them all, that's what Sunday was. Lucky. Some people broke their backs all seven days.

3

Bimby's feet slapped the mud of the dike as he walked to Jesse's hut down in Settlement Number Two. He looked across the rice fields, laced over with ditches and canals. Tomorrow he'd be back in the fields. If he was lucky, he'd be carting the harvest to the mill. That was hard work, but not backbreaking.

A man came toward him, a hulking dark figure. He was one of the drivers. He carried his lash in his left hand. Bimby walked straight, trying not to show fear. As they approached each other, the driver grunted, looking down. Bimby saluted respectfully.

Bimby passed three women with washing on their heads. They were giggling and laughing, in high spirits.

Jesse had a cabin all his own. It was close to the dike and looked toward the landing where he kept his boat. Jesse's boat was a miracle to most people. Jesse had made it before he'd lost his right arm, working on it when he'd finished Massa's work. Nobody knew why Massa let him keep it. He just did. Jesse had cut and shaped the wood. He'd made the boat strong, so it could take rough weather. He had oars for rowing, an oar for sculling and an anchor too. He always carried fishing tackle. Jesse had a mast and a sail for his boat, but the boat wasn't really made for sailing. Needed a keel, Jesse said, like the fin of a shark, but pointing down. He only sailed her before the wind.

People had said Jesse's boat would be stolen. Some fool would try to run away in it. But Jesse kept the oars hidden, the oars and the sail. And most people were afraid of the water—that, and the overseer's musket. On the water a man

was a sitting duck. Anyway where could a black man go?

Jesse was sitting in the doorway nodding, the sun bleaching his battered straw hat. His head came up as Bimby approached. He stretched his legs and stood up slowly. "Time to go, is it, young'un?"

"Don't know, Jesse. You the boss."

"Boss of what?" Jesse winked. "Boss of nothin'." He looked straight at Bimby. "I used to be the boss of all the teamsters: horses, wagons, carriages and all. Now it's Jimmy. Today I'm boss of one tadpole." He smiled and clapped Bimby on the shoulder. "More like a beanpole you're gettin' to be." Jesse looked toward the

landing. There was sadness in his face. "Jimmy, he's takin' *his* boys." Jesse's mouth turned down at the corners. "I'm jus' Massa Butler's clown," he said.

Jesse made Bimby mad. He shouldn't talk that way. Sure, sometimes Massa thought Jesse was funny. But Jesse was tall, broad-shouldered and proud. He wasn't bent much for a man of his years. It was just his white hair that gave his age away. And Massa Butler was a good Massa. Even Ma said she'd heard of plenty worse. Ma said it was Jesse's fault he only had a stub for an arm. He'd lost it from drinking, Ma said, working up in the rice mill, drunk. Ma loved Jesse like Bimby did but Ma was fair-minded. She didn't blame everything on Massa Butler. She even held her tongue about Mr. Wells. Mr. Wells was Ma's overseer. He was mean. Maybe meaner than Bucky even.

Jesse put his hand on Bimby's shoulder. "Cheer up, boy," Jesse said.

Bimby smiled up into Jesse's face. His forehead was high and wide. His eyes were kind.

Jesse's face brightened. "I'll be takin' the reins again today. Just like I did when I was young." Jesse chuckled. "I can drive with the reins between my teeth and hold the whip in my right hand."

Bimby smiled again and made a whipping motion. "We takin' guests in our wagon?"

"No," Jesse said. "We takin' whiskey, food and wine."

"How many folks, Jesse? How many comin' today?"

"How would I know?" Jesse said. "Ask Jimmy that. His boys are drivin' the *people* wagons."

Crazy Mary sat on the rickety pier. She was worthless to Massa but he treated her kind. He didn't send her off with the real old folks. Crazy Mary wasn't worthless to herself. She fished most of the day, grinning and having a high old time. She never caught any fish, least-ways not that Bimby knew of. Mary was ugly. The few teeth she had bucked out and her clothes were always tattered and filthy. But Mary was kind, kind like Jesse, not bitter like Jesse. "How the fish runnin'?" Jesse asked.

"Runnin' too fast," said Crazy Mary.

Jesse undid all his clever knots and set the boat free. Bimby shoved the boat into the shallows and they both stepped in. Bimby took the oars with that little chill of happiness that came with floating. Crazy Mary waved and cackled. The oars took the boat out into the stream. Jesse's arm was strong on the steering oar. He wasn't sculling yet. He set his eyes on the bend in the river. Every time Bimby started out with Jesse, he thought about going on out to sea. He dreamed of rowing downriver out into the Sound, over the ocean waves, straight across to Africa or maybe Spain. But Jesse had told him why they couldn't do that. He'd told him about the sudden storms, how they tossed a boat as if it was a thimble. And Bimby would have known without being told. He'd seen how winter storms had whipped the beach out on Little St. Simons and stripped the roots of the palmetto trees bare.

They passed other landings and a cluster of buildings, the mills, infirmary and overseer's house. Bimby was happy to be on the way. He missed St. Simons. One day, about a year ago, Mr. Wells had told him, "Time to go live with the older boys now. Time to work the fields for Massa Butler."

Bimby knew Ma's hut like he knew his own toes. He knew every tree for a mile around and the Old Mansion House and all. Today they'd take the shell road to a picnic ground. The shell road led past the "Bloody Swamp" where a battle had raged a hundred years ago. It was there invading Spaniards had been defeated. Ma said some of the Spanish had been black.

The tide was with them as they ran down-river, but sweat stood out on Bimby's forehead. He rested on the oars but the boat kept moving even so, not just with the tide, but with Jesse's sculling. Jesse could scull like anything. Sometimes he and Bimby went fishing. Bimby took the line and Jesse made the boat go. Late one Sunday they'd caught six white mullet. Mullet was tastier than catfish, tastier by a million miles.

They rounded a bend and came out from behind a stand of pines. A hawk wheeled and drifted over the rice fields. Buttermilk Sound was just ahead. Bimby looked down at his own arms, skinny but strong. Rowing made them strong. Bimby figured he could row anywhere, but he respected the sea. Jesse's face when he talked about it, that's what made Bimby respect the sea.

Bimby rested again. Today they were bound for Butler Point on the Hampton River. That's where the wagons would start their journey. But in Bimby's mind, he kept on going past Butler Point, curving south to Long Island, just below Little St. Simons. One day Jesse had put him ashore so he could explore Long Island by himself. Bimby remembered his golden moment. He'd stood on a bluff and looked out to sea. He'd given himself to a childish fancy. This was *his* island. He could find fresh water or maybe dig a well. He was smart enough and strong enough to do those things. He'd begun to feel what it was to be free. But Long Island hadn't belonged to Bimby. It might be Massa's for all he knew.

After that, walking north along the shore to meet Jesse, something dark had pressed in on his spirit. It came back to him now for just a minute.

4

Jesse whistled low, jolting Bimby out of his reverie. He was looking toward the north bank of the river. Bimby turned and there he was, the great blue heron, standing in a strip of marsh along the riverbank. Bimby had seen the bird once before. He supposed there might be more than one, but he thought of it as one bird anyway. Bimby whopped the water with one of the oars and the heron slowly unfolded its wings, turned a quarter circle to meet the wind and took deliberately to the air. Bimby watched the bird fly, long legs dangling behind, as it headed for the outer islands. When the bird had become a speck in the blue Jesse said, "Come on now, boy. We have maybe ten more miles to row. We can't let the barges overtake us."

Bimby was already tiring a little. He squinted at the place where the heron had been. "Jesse, where would you fly if you had wings?"

The question seemed to bring Jesse pain. As he started to speak, a familiar shadow passed over his face. "Too late to fly," he said.

Bimby bent to the oars, Jesse sculled, and they moved swiftly south into Buttermilk Sound.

It wasn't until they passed Five Pound, where the overseers sent runaways and other hard cases, that Jesse smiled again. Jesse had been to Five Pound long ago, said it was a rotten swamp, figured he'd keep clear of it, that is, if he could. Sometimes people were sent there for no good reason. Jesse smiled and set his eyes on a point on shore where the Hampton River started. Bimby couldn't see anything but marsh grass and undergrowth reflected in the water but Jesse steered into the opening. Must be high tide. The river was deeper than it was most

times, deeper and clearer. Bimby could see
the dark mud and streaks of gleaming, white
sand. A school of tiny black fish darted away;
a dragonfly hovered, bitter blue in the sun,
then darted off.

Whenever they were going to Butler Point,

they hid the boat up in Turtle Creek. Turtle Creek was their secret.

As they entered the creek, Bimby thought about crocodiles. The banks were muddy and the foliage grew thick, crowding in on both sides. Bimby loved the creek, but it frightened him, too. Reptiles wallowed in places like this. He'd seen crocodiles out on the mudflats, but he knew they must come here too. Sometimes he bad-dreamed about crocodiles.

The creek narrowed and the tips of Bimby's oars touched the shore, fouling in the vines. Bimby shipped the oars, letting Jesse do all the work. They moved silently into a tunnel under arching branches, darkened by leafy flowering vines. Jesse hunched to keep clear of the vines. Bimby leaned out, nearly catching a blossom, almost making the boat capsize. He rocked quickly to the other side. Bimby's antics struck Jesse as funny and he laughed, hooted and laughed some more. "You swim good enough, boy. What's the trouble? You shouldn't be scared of bein' baptized."

Bimby frowned.

"Swimmin' is fine, but not here! That it, boy?"

40

They stepped into the mud and beached the boat at a place where Jesse knew a path began. Not much of a path, Bimby thought. Likely never been traveled by anyone but Jesse and, once in a while, by Bimby too.

Jesse tied the boat to a little tree and they started walking. Bimby didn't like that path. They both watched the ground until they crossed the barren place near the settlement. Bimby followed Jesse past the huts and on uphill to the great live oak where Philip Washington had his praise meetings. Some people had gathered already. Bimby's heart skipped a beat. Was Ma there? He looked sharp at the women in their bright clothes. No. Ma wasn't there, not yet anyway. Bimby hadn't known he and Jesse would come here. Jesse liked to spring surprises. Maybe Bimby wouldn't have to wait. Maybe he could talk to Ma *before* the picnic.

They sat on the ground awhile, resting in the shade of the great tree with its trailing, bluish Spanish moss. Bimby saw his mother join a group of women. She wore a yellow dress that Bimby had never seen before. Ma was always cutting and shaping cloth, making things for herself and others. She said Miss Fanny had

41

started her off. Miss Fanny, she'd been mistress for a spell back when Ma was young, before Bimby was born. Miss Fanny hated slavery. She'd only lived in Georgia four months, but the people had never forgotten her kindness.

Ma didn't see Bimby; at least if she did she gave no sign. Jesse answered the question in Bimby's mind. "No time to visit with your ma now. Besides it wouldn't be fittin' to group with the women. An' we'll be slippin' away before the meetin's over. You and me has to harness up and drive to the landin'. We got to meet Massa and his guests. We got to keep busy this mornin', boy."

Bimby nodded, watching his ma.

Ma saw him now. She nodded and smiled a little. Bimby liked to see Ma dressed up. Today she was wearing a lace collar. Bimby knew that hat. It was straw with a wide brim and fancy flowers, paper flowers, at one side. The other women wore fancy things too, flounces and frills, colored ribbons on bright dresses. Mostly the women's feet were bare.

Old Philip came in and sat on a stump, holding his Bible, pulling at and fussing with his light flowered waistcoat. The flowers were sewn on with fine threads, brocade Ma called it. The waistcoat and Philip's high, white collar were grand but his trousers were ragged and his feet were bare. And his feet were big! Lordy, Philip looked like a duck when he walked.

Old Philip stood up and flip-flopped over to the middle of the clearing. He looked solemnly around the circle, first at the women, then around to Jesse and Bimby. Long tendrils of Spanish moss waved gently over his head. He opened his Bible. Bimby and everyone knew he couldn't read but that never bothered old Philip, not for a minute. He started right off with how it rained for forty days and forty nights. He always started that way but nobody ever got fidgety because nobody knew how he would *end*. His voice rose and trembled. He hustled the animals into the ark and then he got onto Jonah somehow. After that his voice began to sing. Dee-liverance was heavy on his mind.

Bimby caught sight of Jimmy coming up the slope. Jimmy and his boys. Jimmy's barge must have followed closer than Bimby thought. Jimmy was big and handsome and golden-skinned. He swung his shoulders as he walked. Talk was, his father was white. Why did Jimmy have to come to praise meetings? He just came to laugh at Philip Washington. Five of his boys walked behind Jimmy, all familiar to Bimby. Mostly his boys feared Jimmy.

A word from Jimmy and the overseer had a driver whip a boy, with the bull whip that is, not just the lash. If a boy was really sassy, Jimmy had him sent to Five Pound for a spell. Bimby dreaded growing up if it meant being under Jimmy's hand, having him watch his every move. Of course, Bimby might be a carpenter or cooper or maybe a blacksmith like his pa. Jesse said he had the makings of any of those.

Jimmy and his boys sat apart from the others as if they might be too good for praise meetings. Looking at them, Bimby was scared. He couldn't say what it was that scared him. Maybe they all took on Jimmy's meanness. *Meanness,* that was it. That's what frightened Bimby. Meanness in someone who was boss over you. Once Jimmy had said something mean about Jesse, done it on purpose to make Bimby mad. Philip Washington's voice broke into Bimby's thoughts but not for long. Bimby looked at Jesse's face, picked up an acorn and chucked it angrily at a stump.

Jesse whispered, "What's got into you today?"

Bimby's face cleared. "Nothin'," he said. "Just rememberin'."

"Remember somethin' different."

Philip Washington scowled in their direction, then scowled over at Jimmy and his boys. Then he kept going with his prayers.

As Philip finished praying, Bimby felt Jesse's hand on his back, signaling him it was time to go. Bimby was sorry not to stay for the shout. The shout was much the best part. Bimby liked to watch the people sing and clap, loved to watch them going around in a ring. Ma took part sometimes, but she never could lose herself in a shout. She couldn't let the spirit take her in hand.

Jesse and Bimby started moving off. Bimby looked back, raising his hand. His ma nodded, smiling broadly this time. Bimby asked Jesse, "Ma know I'm comin' to see her this evenin'?"

Jesse said, "Sure boy. I told her last week. Old Jesse had this day all planned."

Bimby turned again for a glimpse of his ma. He had a crazy notion he might not see her again. Not ever. Foolishness that's what it was. Seemed he'd been trying to scare himself lately.

45

5

The path took them into a grove of trees. Jesse hurried toward the stable. He wanted to get there before Jimmy. He wanted to have first choice of a horse. One thing about Jesse, he could stand up to Jimmy, sassy as Jimmy was sometimes. Jesse wouldn't take any sass from Jimmy. He'd just call him *boy* and that made Jimmy wild, but something in Jesse took the upper hand, maybe something going back to when Jimmy had been one of Jesse's boys.

Bimby realized he was falling behind. He hurried to catch up to Jesse.

The Mansion House stables were ramshackle even though the Mansion House was fine. Jimmy came up as Jesse led his horse out. Jesse had the best one sure enough. Bimby could tell from the way Jimmy grumbled. Bertha and her girls were fixing up the wagons. She took pride in her work, Bertha did. If the white folks were foolish enough to ride wagons, Bertha could see that the wagons were clean. "We swept these," she told Jesse, "till there isn't a seed or a grain of sand. And *you,*" she said, pointing at Jesse, then rocketing her finger toward the worst wagon, "will carry the food and such in that wagon there."

Jesse had thought the wagons were a joke. There was only one carriage on Butler Point and that one had a broken wheel. Jesse took it as funny that white folks would ride in wagons. He'd told Bimby even Massa rode a wagon to picnics. But, looking at *his* wagon, Jesse didn't think things were funny anymore. He frowned as he backed his horse between the whippletrees. Lordy, Bimby thought, women could be a pain sometimes.

Jesse was a wizard at harnessing a horse to a plow, to a wagon, to any old thing. The fingers

47

of that one hand worked like lightning, but he never seemed to be in a hurry. The lack of an arm made some things harder. Bimby helped him fasten the bellyband. Before Bimby knew it, they were up on the wagon seat and off to the landing. The wagon bumped and joggled over the ruts. The moss hanging from the oaks along the road was thick. Bimby pushed it aside to keep it out of their faces.

There was a flat place by the Mansion House landing, grassy and nice where the earth had been filled in behind a wall. The landing itself was a sturdy pier, new-looking, with fat pilings freshly peeled.

Bimby jumped down. After they teased the horse around and jockeyed the wagon rear-end to the water, Bimby ran out to the end of the pier. An old barge was riding empty in the stream, its bow pointing upriver, its anchor line

taut, the swift water sliding past its sides. That was Jimmy's barge. The tide was running out. Off to the east, Bimby could hear the sound of the sea, or he thought he could. It was faint, like the whisper of a conch shell.

From somewhere upriver came a shout and Bimby saw the first of Massa's twin barges. Jesse came out and watched, too. It was quite a sight, all those backs bent to the oars, the gay awnings flapping at their edges. The lead barge came fast, kicking up curls of white at the bow. Behind it came another, carrying more passengers than the first.

Jesse said, "Lord, look at those black boys pullin' the white folks to their feastin' place. High noon is a murderin' time to row fast. Massa Butler make the boys bend." Jesse made a rhythmic sound in his throat, like oarsmen grunting out their strokes. "He make the boys

keep that beat. His barges move better than any steamboat.''

When the barges drew close things were all a-bustle, the ladies all squealing and carrying on, the gentlemen talking. There was only room to dock one barge at a time. Massa Butler's barge came in first. Massa jumped to the pier. He was fine and dandy in his boots and breeches, in his lace-front shirt open at the collar. He greeted Jesse and nodded to Bimby. Massa reached out and helped a lady come ashore. The oarsmen hopped to it, holding the lines so the barge would stay snug up against the pier, so it wouldn't leave a gap, then close again and maybe crush some pretty ankles.

Jimmy and his boys drove up from the stable in the middle of the fuss. There were three wagons ready for Massa and his guests. One horse snorted out a snootful of dust. The wagons creaked and groaned as Jimmy's boys jumped down. Jimmy was in a good mood, for him. He grunted at Jesse and Bimby and grinned his devilish grin. "Massa got a passel o' ladies today."

Massa's oarsmen and Jimmy's boys unloaded the crates and cases, the barrels of fish, the hams and other goodies. The guests sat on the grassy bank, joking and laughing, in great spirits. Massa watched as Jimmy's boys loaded Jesse's wagon. Bimby helped carry melons. Lordy, there was a lot of stuff.

When they finished, Bimby moved up beside Jesse. Massa spoke to Jesse. He spoke low as if they had a secret. "You go on ahead. No sense waiting." Massa scratched his ear. "On second thought," he said, "wait for us out on the shell road. I'll lead the party."

Massa and Jesse looked into Jesse's wagon, looking to see that things were packed right. Massa took special care about the melons and wine, making sure the cases wouldn't slide around, that the melons were properly wrapped in the blankets. Then Massa went back to join his friends.

Seemed to Bimby that Massa was pretty nice to Jesse. Jesse had no call to complain that he was Massa's clown.

As Bimby and Jesse started off, Massa's barge was being taken out to anchor and the second one was coming in. Jimmy and his boys were standing around, waiting for the folks to board the wagons. Bimby's heart was happy as they joggled along. Off to the east, beyond a broad creek, was another plantation house and sheep meadows sloping down to the water. Bimby watched a small flock moving toward the creek, white woolen spots in all that green.

They passed over a stretch of rutted earth, trees overhead, lots of shade to be thankful for, and came to the shell road. The road ran, almost straight, to the south end of St. Simons Island. Out on the road the sun was blinding, reflecting off the shells of all kinds of mollusks—clams, oysters, scallops and others. Bimby knew shells. His mother had taught him most of the names. Jesse didn't like too many questions but Bimby asked one anyway. "Do you remember Missis? Miss Fanny, Ma calls her."

"Now don't be silly, boy. 'Course I do. Missis had a face jus' like an angel. But she was no prettier than your ma. They made a pair. Your ma, she really loved Missis."

Bimby thought Miss Fanny must have loved Ma, too. She'd taught her so many white folks' graces, reading and writing and fancy sewing.

They moved along maybe half a mile, maybe more, until they came to a salt-smelling creek. A little settlement was just ahead. Jesse jerked around and looked back along the burning white road. There were no wagons in sight. He coaxed the horse along a little into the shade of a good-sized oak, at a place where the shoulder of the road was firm.

"We'll wait for the rest of the party here," Jesse said.

"Fine," Bimby said. "Fine with me, waiting in the shade."

6

Bimby looked up expectantly, wondering what Jesse was thinking about. He liked to hear Jesse talk. Jesse always knew the gossip.

Jesse looked around, then up at the sky. At last he said, "I'm thinkin' of things that build up. They build and build for many a year." Jesse snapped his fingers. "Then they're gone, just like that."

"What kind of things, Jesse?"

Jesse gave Bimby a long look, almost shamed

him he looked so hard. "Bimby," Jesse said, "your ma protected you too much."

Bimby frowned. He looked around, afraid the other wagons might be coming, afraid Jesse might not have time to finish talking. A fly buzzed and Bimby shooed it away. Jesse's silence was more than Bimby could stand. "Well, go on, Jesse. What was it Ma protected me about?"

"Well, you're old enough to know the truth about things."

Lordy, Bimby thought, now he's gonna tell me how babies are made. He waited.

"There's talk there's gonna be an auction soon."

The word *auction* sent a chill through Bimby. He figured he'd lost his pa in an auction. Maybe now he'd lose Ma or Jesse. He tried to keep his voice steady. "You mean *here?* You mean Massa aims to sell his people?"

"Yes, I mean *here.* I don't mean a little auction. One of Massa Couper's boys told me he heard Massa Butler tellin' Massa Couper. And I've had some hints from Massa Butler. He's been gamblin' and losin' up north. He'll be sellin' off *all* his people. That means *you* and your ma and all. Almost no chance you'll go

55

with your ma. No chance at all you'll go with me. I might go north with Massa Butler."

For a minute Bimby hated Jesse. Jesse's words had cut him like a fast lash. He said, "Why you have to go and tell me that, Jesse? It just make me sick. Maybe it's lies. Maybe there isn't a grain of truth in it."

"I told you because I believe it's true. And you're man enough to make yourself ready."

"Why did Massa have to go and gamble?"

Jesse rocked back in the wagon seat, laughing. "For fun, mus' be." Jesse winked. "Seems to me I've seen you drawin' broom straws."

"That's right," Bimby said, still angry. "But that was for doin' or *not* doin' things. Like will Wiley carry water or will I."

Jesse teased, "Now isn't that pretty much the same?"

Bimby didn't rise to the bait, at least not the way Jesse wanted him to. "Pretty much the same," Bimby said. "An' if I was Massa here an' I drew straws for money an' I lost my money I'd sell Ma or maybe *you*. I wouldn't care if I sold you to the meanest Massa. I wouldn't care if he whipped you from dawn to sundown. You'd think that was dandy, wouldn't you, Jesse?"

Jesse's face went dead serious. He gave a long, low whistle. He didn't say a word. He just sat there squinting at the road ahead.

Wagons sounded behind them. Jesse clucked to the mare and his wagon started rolling. Bimby heard a yell, sounded like one of Jimmy's boys, then shouts from the gentlemen and screaming from the lady picnickers.

The wagons weren't just coming. They were barreling toward them, two abreast and one ahead. Jesse whooped to Bimby, "They're racin', boy. The white folks are eggin' them on."

Then Jesse did a thing that took more nerve than anything Bimby had ever seen. Figuring to race the white folks' wagons, he took the reins in his teeth like he'd always talked about but never done. He laid the whip on the horse's back. The wretch almost leaped clean out of her skin. She jerked into a gallop as the other wagons thundered after.

Bimby looked around terrified. The other wagons were gaining on them. The lead wagon rocked from side to side, filled with screaming ladies and howling, laughing gentlemen. That was Massa Butler just behind the driver. He was scowling at Jesse for taking up the road.

Jesse crouched forward and brought the whip

down again. He sure could pick a horse. The mare shot forward like a cannonball. The shoulders of the road grew narrower. Out of the corner of his eye, Bimby saw Massa's wagon gaining. Soon it would pull alongside.

Then Jesse did a thing that was just plain crazy. He started cutting Massa's wagon off. Everybody was raising a hullabaloo. Massa's voice rose above the others. Bimby stiffened. There was a culvert ahead where the road passed

over a finger of swamp. As they approached it the dashing horses bumped each other. Bimby heard a splintering noise. Jesse's wagon bucked upward, taking two wheels clear off the ground. It rocked over sickeningly. For an instant Bimby thought it would come back down, and it would have if the horse had kept going. But she didn't. She panicked and reared and over they went. Bimby flew through the air, hurtling across the shoulder of the road. He landed in a clump of tall swamp grass, followed by a melon bumping down the slope.

Bimby moved his legs to be sure they were sound, crept forward toward the road. Mostly the howling and screaming had stopped but one woman kept on. She screamed, sucked air in and screamed some more. Massa Butler's voice came loud and clear. "Shut up, Millie, for the love of God."

The woman moaned and was silent.

Bimby didn't want to come out of the grass. There was a scuffling by the side of the road. Massa Butler said softly, "My God." Then, a little louder, "Bimby, you there?"

Bimby hadn't thought Massa knew his name, hadn't thought he knew him at all. He held back.

"Bimby?"

Bimby stood up. He couldn't look up at Massa Butler. He stared dazedly after the horse as she galloped down the road. She'd busted out of her traces when the wagon upset. Mr. Wells had made Bimby kill a chicken once. It was like that now, making himself look close at the wagon. It had turned clean over. Its wheels had stopped spinning. Bimby saw Jesse's legs sticking out. He looked up at Massa Butler, then back at Jesse's legs. He stepped up and put his hand on one of the wheels. He pushed it and it started spinning again. Massa Butler was shouting for Jimmy's boys. Jimmy and two others hopped down. Massa pressed his shoulder to the wagon. Bimby took a place near Massa but Jimmy shoved him roughly aside. Slowly the wagon was set on its side. Bimby couldn't look while Massa Butler looked. Jimmy and his boys held the wagon steady. Massa Butler knelt, his back to Bimby, still for a moment. Then he rose up slowly and stood looking down. Jimmy and the others looked down too. Jimmy said, "Damned old fool."

Bimby's voice broke out, almost a sob, "Hush you mouth, you black devil."

Massa Butler said firmly, "Both of you hush."

61

One of the ladies spoke to Massa. "Pierce, have the boys gather up the picnic things. Only one melon I see is broken." She spoke soft and kind of pouty. "Lordy, Pierce, let's go on down to the picnic ground."

Massa gave the lady a cold look.

A gentleman spoke. "Lordy, Pierce, we come all the way down from Savannah."

Bimby looked up at the man's face. It was white and soft. The cheeks were pink. The man was sweating like a butchered pig. His face swam before Bimby's eyes. Bimby was reminded of the quicklime pit over where the men tanned hides. Bimby thought of something that had happened long ago, something he'd forgotten. He remembered standing on the edge of the pit and somebody yelling at him, *Git back, boy!*

He'd never gone near the place again. He'd done his best to forget the awful pit, the sickening stench of animal hides. Bimby thought he must be going mad. The faces were moving but Jesse wasn't moving. Jesse wasn't moving anymore.

7

The blacks were silent. The whites talked
softly. One voice rose above the others, the
voice of the man who came from Savannah.

Bimby gave a little whimper. He broke into
a run along the side of the road, going back
the way they had come. He heard a voice call-
ing his name. He fell headlong, sliding on the
palms of his hands. When he gained his feet
again, he turned in answer to his name. He
wiped his arm across his face. Sweat stung his

eyes. He brought up his shirttail and wiped his eyes clear. It was Massa Butler standing beside the road. "Come back, boy."

Bimby stood.

"You can't walk a shell road with bare feet, boy."

Bimby said nothing. As he moved off again, disobeying Massa, Massa shrugged and turned his back. Bimby sobbed and started running again. He ran fast in the damp slick grass at the edge of the road. He ran until every breath brought pain. He let himself fall in the shade of a tree, but he couldn't stay still, he couldn't stop going. He inched forward on the grass, crawling as if he had lost his legs, edging forward with his arms. He struggled to his knees, gained his feet again and moved ahead. A quarter mile or so farther on, a big snake was sunning in the middle of the road. Bimby barely noticed. Jesse had taught him which ones were poison but Bimby didn't even look close at this one. The islands are made of the skeletons of snakes, that's what Jesse had said.

Bimby frightened two pale blue moths. They fluttered over the road ahead. Up and down and around in a crazy pattern, off into the underbrush.

The shoulder narrowed and the road became a causeway with swamp on either side. Bimby shifted over to the middle of the road. He'd always thought his feet were tough but now, as

he ran, they burned like all the fires of hell. He pressed on into the shimmering heat. The road was a liquid blur of white and, just there ahead, was that a parting of the trees? Could that be where the dirt road started? Bimby fell again and dragged himself along as he had before. He lay still a moment. Were there hoofbeats sounding on the road? Silence, except for the sounds of the swamp.

Bimby struggled to his feet and made his way back to the grassy shoulder. Again he fumbled for his shirttail, wiped his eyes and stuffed his shirttail in. One of the sleeves of his shirt was torn. He stared at it, the shirt his ma had made. He stared at the gaping, tattered sleeve. He moved trembling into the shade. Yes, this was the place. There the dirt road tunneled through the brush and trees, curving out of sight a few yards along. He stared down at his sleeve again and shuddered. He ran blindly along the road, ran into the settlement and past the place where Old Philip had preached. There was no one about. He ran down a slope through a stand of stunted oaks straight to Ma's hut and bolted through the door. "Ma, it's Bimby."

There was no answer.

"Ma," he wailed.

Distant voices babbled outside. Bimby tried to see but the sun had burned his vision away. He backed against the wall, cupped his hands and covered his eyes. Lights flashed and swam, all different colors. He took his hands away from his face. Someone stood black against the light in the doorway. Bimby took an uncertain breath. "Ma?"

"Bimby, that you?"

Bimby tried to breathe steady but his breath came fast. He couldn't stop his chest from heaving. His ma moved over and sat on her cot. Bimby stumbled forward and clutched her knees. He put his face in her lap and sobbed as he had sobbed when he was little.

Ma was quiet until he was still. "What is it, Bimby?"

Bimby's voice shook. "I tore the shirt you made me, Ma. Right here." he said, picking at the sleeve.

"Tell me later if you want to, Bimby."

"I told you, Ma."

"Come now, Bimby, settle down."

Bimby got up off his knees. He stood straight.

The room spun at first; then his vision cleared. He could see Ma's face, dim in the gloom. Bimby moved over and looked out the doorway. The cabin was on a gentle rise. Bimby remembered. He knew every stone and growing thing. This place *was* home. Skunk cabbage grew in that little glade and jack-in-the-pulpit just down there. A bird twittered in the underbrush, twittered and fussed among the blossoming vines. Another bird, bright as fire, streaked across the grass. Bimby said, "Jesse's dead, Ma."

"Bimby, you sure? Why, he was at the praise meetin'. . . ." Her voice trailed off.

Bimby turned back. He said, "Our wagon turned over. Jesse started racin' with white folks' wagons. . . ."

"You all right, Bimby? You break any bones?"
Bimby didn't answer.

Ma said gently, "Jesse was close to the end of his life."

Close? What did that mean? Everybody was close. He said, "Jesse's not the first person I've seen dead. Remember, Ma? You remember when Billy Tobias drowned. I saw his ma carry him up the path."

"That's right, Bimby."

"Well, Billy drowning didn't tell me much."
Ma waited.

"It just scared me. It made me think how it would feel to *be* dead."

Ma hugged herself as if she had a chill. She got up and stood patiently, facing Bimby.

Bimby was suddenly mad at Ma. She didn't grieve. She didn't understand. What was the sense in talking at all? What could she say that would make any difference? Bimby clenched his fist and turned away, turned back to the doorway again.

Ma's voice came soft and lonely. "Bimby, everybody got to die."

Bimby covered his eyes again. The lights came back, same as before. He swayed a little.

Ma said, "Bimby, you better lie down."

He moved unsteadily to the cot. Ma went and sat down on her doorstep.

Bimby fixed his eyes on a dark corner. He thought, *Jesse didn't die. Somebody killed him. No, Jesse killed himself. But why?*

Bimby made himself look away from the corner. Ma was quiet. Bimby looked past her, fixing his eyes on black tree branches. He had to stop thinking crazy. *Jesse was killed by accident.*

But he was racing to show off to Massa Butler, pretending he wasn't old anymore. And he was racing like a man who didn't care. Life hadn't meant much to Jesse anymore. Bimby's heart thumped a hundred to the minute. He listened while it slowed down.

8

When Bimby woke, it was dim outside. Ma
was still sitting on the doorstep. She was looking
toward the dark trees. For a moment, Bimby
thought he had never gone away, never left the
hut where he had grown up. Then it all came
back to him in a flood. Bimby stirred and his
ma turned. "You slept sound, Bimby."

"That's right, Ma."

Bimby lay back, staring into the dark. The
peepers chirped in the nearby swamp. A woman

was singing her baby to sleep. Bimby heard the steady call of the mourning dove. The sounds were all part of him. Sleepy sounds. Two stars winked in the darkening sky.

Ma got up from the doorstep and sat on a backless wooden chair. She leaned forward, trying to see Bimby's face, then went to the table and lit a candle. Candles were special, not for every night.

Neither spoke for what seemed a long time. Bimby's voice broke the quiet. He said, "Where did Pa go when he was sold?"

Bimby's ma stiffened. She said, "Lordy, boy."

"Jesse said you protected me from things too much. That was one of the last things Jesse said."

Ma sounded frightened. "What kind of things, Bimby?"

"One thing was about the auction. Have you heard Massa aims to sell his people?"

Ma nodded and sighed softly.

Bimby said, "Ma, I want to go find Pa."

Ma drew in a sharp breath. "Don't be foolish, Bimby."

"You better tell me if you know where he is. I aim to go lookin' anyway."

72

The sounds of evening came clear again. At last Ma spoke. She said, "Your pa was lookin' for freedom, Bimby."

Bimby asked breathlessly, "Did Pa run away?"

Ma was silent again, half a minute or so. "Yes, he did, Bimby, but they brought him back."

Bimby could feel his heart pounding again.

"He was flogged within an inch of his life. Then they took him to Five Pound. Didn't take him long to die. I should have told you long ago. But you had bad dreams enough without bad-dreamin' about your pa."

Bimby didn't know why, but he wasn't surprised. He turned his head away, searching out the stars. Now, sitting up, he could see only one. He watched it for a long time. He faced his ma with level eyes. "Ma, I got to follow Pa."

"Your pa's dead, Bimby."

"I got to follow him anyway."

"Sleep on it, Bimby. Decide tomorrow."

"I already slept."

Ma's voice was steady and quiet. "Your pa and I were better off than most. You know that, Bimby. Your pa had a skill. He was respected. Miss Fanny taught me things. And I taught *you*. We raised ourselves up a little. But it didn't make us happy bein' better off. It made us yearn. Miss Fanny talked to me about freedom, about people in the north who pondered freedom for us down here. Black men too, *free* black men respected by black and white alike. There are many men who want to put an end to slavery. Did you know that, Bimby?"

"No, Ma. You should have told me."

"I wanted you to grow up happy. Discontent in a boy makes a sour man. No sense in a man bein' sour. Take Mr. Wells. Mr. Wells is white and free, but Mr. Wells sour all the same."

Bimby nodded.

"Escapin's hard and risky, Bimby."

"Seems like I'll die if I don't go, Ma. Seems like I thought about it all my life, thought without knowin' I was thinkin'."

Ma's eyes gleamed in the yellow light. She spoke softly. "I thought about it too. But I never reckoned you'd have a chance." She looked straight into Bimby's eyes, with pain and longing. She started to speak and fell silent.

At last she said, "Go and scout around a little. Make sure there's no listeners."

Bimby went to the door. The woman wasn't singing to her baby anymore. Another was moaning in a hut close by, not loud, just moaning herself to sleep. Bimby looked up. The

night was clear, millions of stars. A tree stood at the corner of the hut. It was smaller than he remembered. Bimby laid his hand on the bark, then on the mud and shell wall of the hut. The feel of the shells reminded him of something. He felt the soles of his feet. They were tough and crusty like tanned leather, but they'd been cut up by the shell road. He walked around back, looking off toward a cluster of huts that lay between him and a stand of trees. He looped around Ma's hut, listening and watching, and went back in. Ma was fussing over the table, putting things in a kerchief.

Bimby said, "Nobody snoopin'. If we listen, we can hear if someone snoops."

Bimby sat on the edge of the cot.

"When your pa made plans to go north I told him things Miss Fanny had told me. When she was fixin' to leave, she gave me the names of people up north, as if she knew someday I'd need them."

"Seems like everybody leaves you, Ma."

Ma showed an angry face. She rummaged in her things on the corner shelf and brought out a piece of paper. Looked like a leaf torn out of a book. She studied it, tilting it toward the candlelight. She looked away again, out the doorway, a melancholy stare. "Your pa had doubts about running away. Seems like his heart was split in two."

"My heart isn't split. It really isn't, Ma."

"Well, the only way I know is go down the coast. I guess you'll be takin' Jesse's boat."

Bimby nodded.

"Go down the coast to Jacksonville. Mostly the islands will protect you from the sea. Stay inside the islands as much as you can. St. Andrew Sound, that's the second place that's open to the sea. It might be rough, if the sea is rough. The town of Brunswick down there on St. Andrew Sound. You shouldn't go in too close to Brunswick. Keep away from towns."

"I can beach the boat if the sea is rough. I'll wait for times when the sea is calm."

"You can make it safe if you do that. And mostly wait for an incoming tide."

"Ma, how will I know when I come to Jacksonville?"

"Jacksonville's on the St. Johns River. After that river you got no place else to go. You got to go inland or out to sea. There's no more islands to hide behind. And if you wait awhile, you'll see big ships goin' in and out. Pa said Jacksonville's fifty miles or more from here. Take your time. Go careful. It might take a week, maybe more.''

"Am I free when I get to Jacksonville, Ma?"

"Lord, no, boy.''. She smiled faintly, looking at the paper in her hand. "Thank the Lord I taught you to read."

Bimby thought he heard a sound outside. Ma grew tense. She blew out the candle. "Candlelight might draw Mr. Wells."

Bimby's ma went on. "Jacksonville's where you take your chances. Wait until the tide is running in, but not too fast. Then row yourself into Jacksonville harbor. Remember this now, Bimby. Look for ships at anchor. Don't go to the docks. Read the names painted on the ships. Find one from Boston if you can. New York will do, or Philadelphia. Those three are written on the paper. Those are the biggest and safest too." Ma paused. "But all the people in them don't want us to be free."

Bimby listened. Nothing out there now but familiar sounds.

His ma went on. "Hail someone on the deck of the ship you choose. Tell him you must

78

speak to the ship's captain. Wait for him if he isn't on board. Speak *only* to the ship's captain. When you meet him, look him right in the eyes. If you trust him, ask him if he'll take you north. Tell him you'll work to pay your passage. Say you want to go to work in the north. If you don't trust him, pretend you got on the wrong ship. Make up another captain's name. Tell him you're looking for a captain from a different city. Say you're looking for so-and-so to give him a message.''

Bimby's ma lit the candle again. She put a spoon and a bowl of corn mush on the table. ''Eat your fill,'' she said. She put the paper on the table. ''The names on that list, the ones under the city names, are people to trust. Most names are just family names. Anyone in those families will help you for sure. Miss Fanny told me that. One or two are the names of special people to trust, if those people are still alive.''

Bimby looked at the list and tried to say the names. Ma helped him. ''Your pa had all those names by heart. You learn them by heart when you have a chance.''

Bimby studied the paper, learning how to say the names. Ma sat on the steps and listened.

When he could say them all she turned her face into the night.

She stood up. Her voice had hardened. "The things in the kerchief will keep you for a while. You can eat shellfish if you run out of food. Only thing is, the salt will make you thirsty. Take my gourd for drinkin' water. Make the food and water stretch as long as you can."

Bimby's voice trembled. "I will, Ma."

He took the gourd off its peg on the wall. He knotted up the corners of the cloth, leaned over and blew out the candle. His ma went and stood by the cot. Bimby moved toward the doorway. He heard the cot creak as his ma lay down. "Bimby," she said softly, questioning.

"Yes, Ma."

"Nothin', boy," she whispered.

Bimby thrust himself into the night.

9

He stopped at the well and filled the gourd, moved through the outskirts of the settlement, keeping to the shadows. He crossed the barren ground, plunged into the blackness of the swampy woodland. Everything in the path became a snake. Bare roots, stones, everything. He ran in terror, nearly letting the gourd and kerchief fall. That scared him more than snakes. If he lost food and water, he couldn't go far.

He clutched the things tighter than before.

He walked slowly now, trying hard to forget snakes. He took a wrong turning, got away from the path and frightened a tremendous bird. The thing flapped up wildly from the underbrush. Bimby stopped dead in his tracks, thought a minute and retraced his steps. He never had done much walking at night. Black folks were supposed to stay put after dark.

He shivered as he approached the creek. There, just ahead, the water reflected the night sky. He beat back the underbrush that hid the boat. His chest started heaving again. He stood still, trying to steady himself. He gave three convulsive sobs, stowed his bundle and freed the boat from the little tree. In a burst of anger, he shoved the boat into the water, stepped in and drifted a moment before he took up the sculling oar. He sculled gently, ducking constantly to clear vines. A measure of happiness came to him now. Someday he would be as big as Jesse. He imagined for a moment he *was* Jesse, even imagined he had only one arm.

When he got to the river, he saw that the tide was coming in. It was running fast. *Like Crazy Mary's fish,* he thought with a smile. Might not ever see Crazy Mary again, Crazy

Mary or Wiley or anyone else. He didn't dare think of Ma.

The boat moved fast with the tide. He soon cleared the trees on the river's south bank. The night was lighter than before. Bimby saw why. A slice of moon poked above the gentle marsh grass. He looked up at the sky, feeling big inside, his spirit quiet in the stillness. He had never been his own captain. Not until now. He dipped the oars and feathered them as Jesse had done. He wished he could row looking forward, that way sculling was better, but soon he was glad he was looking back. He heard the sound first, a kind of singing. Then he saw it, a black shape moving on the river. He caught his breath. It must be a barge, maybe taking Jesse's body back to Butler Island.

Bimby steered in toward shore. There was tall grass there, but not thick enough to hide the boat while it was still in the water. He chose a tall patch and steered straight in as fast as he could row. The boat bumped the mud, raising its bow. Lordy, that would never do. The helmsman or an oarsman was sure to see the boat. Bimby jumped frantically into the shallow water, sinking deeply into the mud. He pulled at the bow but the boat wouldn't budge. Finally, despairing, he pushed the boat back into the water, hoping the grass would be tall enough to hide it, hoping luck would be on his side.

The singing came louder, something like the sound Jesse had made when they'd watched the oarsmen row toward the Mansion House landing. Bimby held the boat so it wouldn't drift away. He held it still. If they saw him now his chance would be gone, lost forever. He could tell them he'd stood aside to let them pass, that he was on the way back to Butler Island. That way they wouldn't whip him but they'd take him in tow. And, of course, they'd take Jesse's boat away. Bimby stood in the mud, hunching over so as not to be seen. He prayed silently, nearly as strong as Philip Washington.

Bimby could hear the dipping of the oars. The men were really singing now, a kind of dirge. They must be taking Jesse back.

Bimby squinted through the grass, waiting. The barge hove into view. The water was silver from the rising moon, the barge black and moving fast. Bimby held his breath. The singing came loud, a heartbreaking, mournful rhythm, grew faint as the barge disappeared from view.

Bimby waited to be sure nobody else was coming. He pushed the boat back out of the grass. He hoisted himself slowly over the stern. He looked up and down the river before he dipped the oars.

Buttermilk Sound was quiet as a lake, rippled by only a light breeze. The moonlight tipped the ripples silver. If he rowed north, up Buttermilk Sound, he would find himself back at

Butler Island. He could pay his last respects to Jesse. Once he turned south he was a runaway. No turning back. That was the best way to please old Jesse. Jesse had said, *Too late to fly.* Well, not for Bimby. And what was he flying *from* anyway? Hell, that's what. Better to be dead than have your spirit cut to ribbons.

He pulled hard on the starboard oar and fell into a steady stroke, going south.

FURTHER NOTE

Actress and writer Frances Anne Kemble, called "Miss Fanny" and "Missis" by the Butler slaves, was born in England in 1809. The Kembles were a family of actors and Fanny's father, Charles, was a gifted Shakespearean player. Fanny started her career shortly before her twentieth birthday in the role of Juliet at Covent Garden. She was a popular success, though she disliked the stage.

Three years later, she came to America with her father and spent two seasons acting, mostly in New York but also in Boston, Philadelphia, Baltimore and Washington. In June of 1834, she married Pierce Mease Butler of Philadelphia whose family, unknown to Fanny, were slave-owners.

In the winter of 1838-1839, with her husband and their two daughters, one of whom was three and the other an infant, Fanny lived on the Butler plantation in Georgia. She had long since set her mind against slavery and a firsthand view of that institution sharpened her opposition to it.

Fanny went alone to England in 1841. In 1843, after several periods of separation, she wrote her husband seeking a reunion. "For God's sake and for your children's sake . . . let us be wise before it is too late. . . ." Butler chose to ignore her plea and they were divorced in 1849. In our time Fanny would, as a matter of course, have kept her children, but her daughters grew up in their father's house.

Fanny Kemble's *Journal of Residence on a Georgian Plantation in 1838-1839* provided most of the background material for *Bimby*. The 1838-1839 journal was first published in 1863. Especially useful was the 1961 edition edited and with an introduction by John Anthony Scott. The letters of Robert Gould Shaw, written on St. Simons Island during the Civil War, were also useful, as were general works on the subject of slavery in America. Shaw had met Fanny Kemble in his youth and, during his brief stay on St.

Simons, met and talked to people who had been Butler's slaves.

The Georgia and north Florida coasts have changed since the 1850's. The best maps of the period show an almost unbroken protected waterway from Buttermilk Sound to Jacksonville.

The auction mentioned in the story did, in fact, take place. Most of Butler's slaves went under the hammer in 1859. A reporter for the New York *Daily Tribune* described the auction. Families were broken up and sales were made to rough men from the "back river and swamp plantations." Pierce Butler walked among the people he had known and presented each with a silver dollar. It was a weeping day indeed.

The author thanks the New York Public Library for the use of the Frederick Lewis Allen Memorial Room where this book was written. Thanks especially to Alice Bethke and to the staffs of the American History Division and the Map Division.

P.B.

About the Author

PETER BURCHARD is a professional writer and illustrator. He has illustrated close to 100 books. is author of *North by Night, Jed* (chosen as a Notable Book by the American Library Association), *Stranded: A Story of New York in 1875* and *One Gallant Rush* (a scholarly biography). His work has been widely acclaimed. The New York *Times* describes him as having "a splendid facility for characterization." He was a Guggenheim Fellow in 1966.

BIMBY grew out of his long-standing interest in American slavery and the antislavery movement. The story came to him while he was working on another book about an entirely unrelated subject. He says of BIMBY, "It was written out of love, not to meet a need. If it meets a need so much the better."

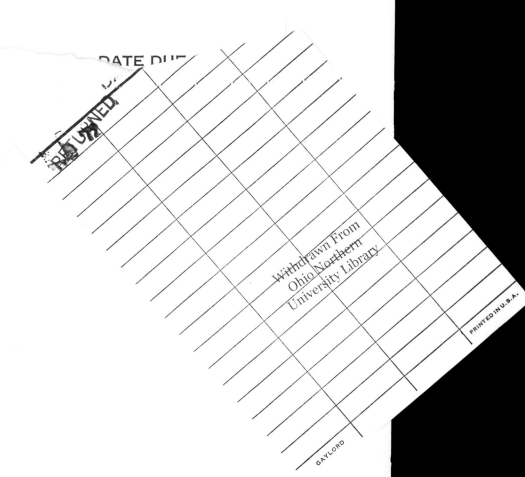